THE EAST PUDDING CHRONICLES
The First Christmas

To Billie,
Merry
Christmas !

CR. Berry

X

The East Pudding Chronicles

THE FIRST CHRISTMAS

WRITTEN BY

CHRISTOPHER BERRY

ILLUSTRATED BY EMILY HARPER

Printed in the UK by Lulu.com

ISBN 978-1-326-46164-5

For Granny
Your candle still burns

THE EAST PUDDING CHRONICLES
The First Christmas

Chapter One
Granny Tells a Story

Another Christmas Eve had come to the village of Dandiest Pug. George and Georgina were one year older, but their love of Christmas – and their excitement for the big day – had not faded a smidge.

Tinsel, mistletoe, Christmas cards, candles, snowglobes and singing snowmen surrounded them as they sat in front of the TV wrapping some last-minute presents. Gentle flecks of light from the fairy lights on the Christmas tree danced across their faces, and the fairy on top smiled down at them.

Tim Burton's *The Nightmare Before Christmas* was on the TV and George and Georgina were humming along to Jack Skellington singing "What's this?" as he explored Christmas Town. Granny was looking after them while Mum and Dad were out for Christmas Eve drinks. She was in her armchair sipping sherry and rubbing Dipstick's tummy. The cute little dog had fallen asleep in her lap, tongue hanging out.

They'd already had tea and baked cakes. Now, with Mum and Dad out, George and Georgina had a chance to wrap some presents for them.

George had bought Mum some candles and a music box with his pocket money. Georgina had painted her a picture of Bumfy the comfy chair from Granny's Christmas stories and framed it.

They had bought Dad some socks, because all of his had holes in them. They'd also bought him a chocolate orange and some Turkish Delight – his favourites – but they hadn't told Mum about those.

"Your father's getting a bit porky," Mum had said a month ago. "No chocolate this Christmas!"

Okay, so Dad's tummy was starting to look a little bit like a watermelon, but how could they deny him a chocolate orange and Turkish Delight?

They wrapped each present the same way. They put the socks, the candles and the chocolates into gift boxes, wrapped the boxes in colourful paper, and tied each one with a ribbon, making a pretty bow on top. Then they slipped each present under the Christmas tree. Georgina looked up at the fairy on top and smiled, because she knew the presents would be safe with her watching over them. She didn't see the fairy wink back at her.

As they put the presents under the tree, George wondered about something, and turned to face Granny.

"Granny, why do we —?" George started to ask.

The front door opened. Mum and Dad were home early from their Christmas Eve drinks. They took off their coats and came into the living room.

"Evening, my darlings!" said Mum cheerily. "How are we all?"

"We're just lovely, thank you," said Granny. "Cakes have been made, Dipstick's been fed and last-minute presents have been wrapped. I believe George was just about to ask me something..."

"Yes," said George. "On the subject of presents... well, it does seem like giving and receiving presents is one of the most important parts of Christmas. But you've never told us why we do it."

"You know, George, you're right," said Granny. "All these years I've been telling you where our Christmas traditions come from, how they all started in the village of East Pudding a long, long time ago. I've told you why Santa visits us, why we kiss under the mistletoe, why we pull Christmas crackers and why we put up Christmas trees. But the one thing I haven't told you is where Christmas itself comes from. How Christmas began."

"Christmas itself?" said Mum. "I don't think even I've heard this story!"

"No, my dear, you haven't," said Granny, smiling. "Gather round, everyone. I have one final story to tell."

So this time Mum and Dad went to sit on the floor at Granny's feet to listen to the story. George sat down in Mum's lap, Georgina sat down in Dad's, and Dipstick lay down in the middle.

And Granny began, "This is the story of the first Christmas..."

Chapter Two
The Lady of the Skies

Once upon a time, there lived a powerful creature made of light, air, dust and magic called the Lady of the Skies. As her name would suggest, she lived above the clouds, watching over the world and looking after the skies and those who inhabited it. She looked after pterodactyls, dragons, BooBoos, eagles, owls, ravens, doves and many other birds and flying creatures. And she had two children to help her. One of them was called Mumble, and the other was called Murmur.

"Wait – what?" said George, interrupting Granny's story and staring at his sister with wide eyes. "Mumble and Murmur were brother and sister?"

"Indeed they were, my darling," said Granny with a grin. "Just like you and Georgina."

"They can't be!" Georgina cried. "They absolutely hate each other! Okay, so sometimes I feel like punching George on the nose when he's annoying, but he's still my brother!"

"Maybe something terrible happened between them..." wondered George. "Maybe it's something to do with this 'West Pudding' place that Granny keeps mentioning in her stories."

"Now, George, sweetheart, are you going to tell this story, or am I?" said Granny with a raised eyebrow.

"Sorry, Granny!" replied George sheepishly.

Granny carried on...

Mumble and Murmur lived with their mother above the clouds for a very long time, helping her to look after the skies. For many thousands of millions of years, there was peace. Then, when humans started appearing on the land below, the Lady of the Skies saw that they were going to be a bit of a handful. These new creatures were very strong-minded. They had beautiful dreams, big imaginations and grand ideas. But they were also prone to doing really horrible things to each other and to the world around them.

The Lady of the Skies decided that she would send Mumble and Murmur to look after the humans on the land, in order to keep them in check. So she turned Mumble and Murmur into humans. Well, humans with magic powers. The first humans lived in two villages called East Pudding and West Pudding. She sent Mumble to look after East Pudding, and Murmur to look after West Pudding.

For many years, Mumble and Murmur ruled over the two villages in peace and harmony. But Mumble and Murmur lived in different ways. Mumble, because he knew what humans were capable of, decided not to get too close to them. He didn't want to be influenced by them. So he visited his people occasionally, not too often, and spent most of his time in his castle. He brought pots, pans, jars, spoons, chairs and clocks to life with his powers to keep him company.

But Murmur thought it best to get to know her people and befriend them. She invited the residents of West Pudding for tea at her castle on lots of occasions, and she spent a lot of time mingling with people in the village.

Over time, this started to change her. Some of the people she made friends with were bad, selfish, didn't care about others, and hurt people in order to make themselves more powerful. They taught Murmur how to lie, cheat, steal – and kill. Not everyone was like this, of course. In fact, most people were pleasant and kind. But Murmur couldn't tell who was nasty and who was nice. She tried to be friends with everyone.

But the selfishness and cruelty of the bad people she'd made friends with started to rub off on her. She became more and more like them.

Once, when she visited Mumble in East Pudding, she decided that her brother's village was better than hers. It hadn't occurred to her before, but the residents of East Pudding seemed to have bigger houses and bigger gardens than the residents of West Pudding. Mumble's castle was taller than her own. And the flowers in East Pudding were prettier than the flowers in West Pudding.

"Brother, your village is better than mine," Murmur said to Mumble outright. "I'm not happy about that."

"I think you're seeing things, darling sister," said Mumble. "Your village is equally wonderful."

"No, brother, it's not. And I don't want it to be equally wonderful, anyway. I want it to be better."

"Why?" asked Mumble. "Why this sudden obsession with being better?"

"Because," said Murmur flatly.

"What an excellent reason!" cried Mumble sarcastically.

Murmur huffed and said quietly to herself, "You'll see, brother. You'll see."

She was hatching a plan. Seeing East Pudding had made her feel inferior, and she didn't like that feeling. She wanted to be better than her brother.

She invited crows and vultures to come and live in West Pudding and be her servants. She had heard that crows and vultures could be ruthless. That's exactly what she needed them to be. She ordered them to fly to East Pudding and raid the village. She told them to steal anything valuable they could find and bring it all to West Pudding.

The crows and vultures flew to East Pudding that night, sneaking into people's houses through open windows and down chimneys. They stole sparkly necklaces, rings and brooches, took food from people's larders, and emptied their cupboards.

They broke into the East Pudding Bank and flew away

with great big bags of gold and silver coins. Meanwhile, other crows and vultures pulled up crops from the fields and stole fruits from the trees.

Worse still, Murmur had given her twisted tree root-shaped magic wand to one of the vultures. This vulture's job was to wave the wand over the crop fields. As it did, the wand rained down a flurry of silver dust. It actually looked really pretty – except that the dust was deadly, and once it had sunk into the soil, it poisoned the land, ensuring that no new crops could grow.

Before anyone in East Pudding had noticed, the crows were flying back towards West Pudding and Murmur with their loot.

After this happened, the people of East Pudding couldn't recover. The village was in tatters and all their money, food and valuables were gone. They became poor and hungry. Mumble did what he could, but he couldn't create something from nothing. His powers didn't work like that.

Meanwhile, the people of West Pudding became filthy-rich. As soon as Murmur handed out the stolen items, the people had so much money that they all made their houses bigger, and so much food that they all started to get a little fat. Murmur had her castle knocked down and rebuilt so that it was taller than Mumble's, and laughed triumphantly as the final piece of stone was laid.

His village struggling, Mumble decided to pay his sister a visit in West Pudding to ask for help.

"Please, dear sister," said Mumble. "A flock of birds descended on East Pudding and ransacked it, making off with all our money and food. My people can't eat. I need your help to rebuild my village."

"Sorry, brother," Murmur hissed. "Mother asked me to look after West Pudding and she asked you to look after East Pudding. It's not my job to help you out. You have to do it yourself."

"Mother would want you to help me," said Mumble.

"Mother isn't here right now," Murmur spat. "Go home,

brother. Sounds like your people need you."

"I'm not your brother," Mumble said quietly under his breath. "Not anymore."

"What? Don't mumble, Mumble!"

"I said, I'm not your brother and you're not my sister. I won't let you forget this."

"Goodbye, Mumble."

As Mumble left Murmur's castle and went back to East Pudding, the air turned suddenly cold, after an eternity of warmth. A frozen wind swirled through the land, chilling Mumble to the bone. Winter had come – for the first time ever.

You see, the Lady of the Skies controlled the weather. Her moods shaped and influenced it. When she was happy and content, the sun shone brightly, and her tears of joy would fall as warm rain all over the land. When she was angry, great storms of thunder and lightning would erupt.

Now, the first winter had arrived. The air was cold and the sky had gone dark and grey. A flurry of something different began to fall from the sky. Something cold landed on Mumble's nose. A fluffy white crystal. A frozen raindrop. A snowflake.

These were not tears of joy. The Lady of the Skies was crying because of what her daughter, Murmur, had done. These were tears of sorrow.

She cried and cried. And it snowed and snowed.

Chapter Three
The Potter Sisters

On the corner of West Pudding, three sisters lived with their parents, Mr and Mrs Potter, in a big house with *lots* of bedrooms. More than they needed, actually. But Mr and Mrs Potter were rich enough to have lots of space.

The three sisters were called Maz, Mary and Chris. Maz was short for Marianne, and Chris was short for Christina. All three of them lived happy, comfortable lives. They had plenty of clothes, plenty of food, plenty of books and plenty of toys. Plenty of everything, in fact. But they weren't greedy. They were just used to it.

Maz was probably the messiest person in the world. A complete scruff-bag. Her clothes were always ripped and covered in food stains. Her face was always dirty and her hair was always tangled. And her bedroom was the untidiest room in the house. No matter how many times Mr and Mrs Potter told Maz to clean her room and tidy herself up, it just never seemed to go in.

Mary was a plump girl. She loved her food and was particularly fond of cake. Her mother told her she needed to cut back and lose a bit of weight, but that was easier said than done. Mary had a VERY sweet tooth.

Chris was a very sweet little girl. And yes, I mean little. *Very* little. Even though she was older than Maz by one year and older than Mary by two years, her head only came up to their tummies. Being so short made Chris a timid and quiet girl. So often people just didn't see or notice her, and on more than a few occasions she'd been accidentally sat on. Always a painful experience, given that most of the people in West Pudding were quite fat.

On December 24th, Maz, Mary and Chris were sitting in their living room and looking out of the window. They had just enjoyed an enormous roast lunch with all the trimmings, and a treacle sponge for pudding. They were all stuffed. Well, apart from Mary, who was now tucking into a chocolate cake.

"Why does it never stop snowing, Mother?" Maz asked Mrs Potter, who was sitting by the fire reading a book.

"I don't know, sweetheart," Mrs Potter said. "It has been snowing a lot, hasn't it?"

"It's been snowing for years, Mother," Mary said with a mouthful of cake. "A few hours every day. I can't remember the last time I saw the grass through the snow that's covering it."

"Well, I'll tell you what I think it is," Mrs Potter said, closing her book. "I think someone up there in the sky is really upset and won't stop crying. And all the snowflakes are tears."

"Tears?" Maz said, raising her eyebrow. "That's silly. People don't live in the sky."

"Not people like us, no."

A short while later, Mrs Potter went to make some tea. Mary, Maz and Chris continued to look out of the window and wonder about the snow.

"Do you think Mother's right?" asked Chris in her teeny, tiny voice. "Do you think there's really someone up there crying?"

24

"I know a way we can find out," said Maz with a naughty grin.

"How?" asked Mary.

"Come with me."

Chapter Four
Up the Sky Tree

Maz, Mary and Chris snuck out of the house while Mrs Potter was busy making tea and Mr Potter was fast asleep (and snoring) in his study. Boots crunching, Chris and Mary followed Maz through the thick snow.

Maz took her sisters to a very tall tree that stood on the edge of Pudding Woods, the woods Queen Murmur had told everyone never to go into. The tree was so tall that the top of it was above the clouds. Maz called it the Sky Tree.

"Follow me," said Maz. "Let's climb."

Chris was nervous, shaking and chewing on her lip the entire way up the tree. But she didn't want her sisters to leave her on her own at the bottom, so she didn't have much choice. Mary was excited, but a little bit concerned that she would run out of biscuits. She had stuffed a packet into her dress for the journey, but halfway up the tree, she'd already eaten three quarters of it. Maz was way ahead of her sisters. She had never climbed to the top of the Sky Tree before, so she scrambled up the tree like a monkey, keen and fast, ripping even more holes in her already tatty dress.

The Sky Tree went further into the clouds than Maz expected. Eventually, when she reached the top, Maz placed her foot onto the nearest cloud, realizing that it was so thick she could actually walk on it.

"What are you doing?!" shouted Mary in horror when she reached the top and saw her sister standing on a cloud. "You're going to plunge to your death!"

"No, I'm not!" said Maz. "Come and see! The clouds are thick enough to walk on up here!"

Mary stepped onto one of the clouds and – to her surprise – didn't fall through.

Chris reached the top of the Sky Tree. She saw that her sisters were jumping from cloud to cloud, laughing.

Terrified, Chris stepped onto the cloud nearest to her. Weird, she thought. It was like stepping onto a huge marshmallow. She saw that Maz and Mary were heading further into the distance and she needed to catch up to them.

She walked to the edge of the cloud and prepared to jump onto the next one.

Heart pounding, Chris shut her eyes tightly and launched her little body from the cloud.

But she was too small, and her jump wasn't big enough. She didn't make it to the next cloud and plunged through the gap between them, tumbling through the air.

"Aaaahhhh!!!" Chris screamed.

Maz and Mary spun round and saw their sister falling like a stone through the sky. "Chris – noooo!!" they screamed.

Suddenly, before she knew what was happening, Chris felt a powerful gust of wind hit her from below and blow her upwards. The great wind scooped up Chris into its invisible arms, lifting her up through the sky and dropping her onto one of the clouds near her sisters.

"Chris! Chris! Are you alright?" shouted Maz, who jumped onto Chris's cloud and bent down to hug her.

"I – I d-d-don't like it up here!!" Chris spluttered, sobbing, shaking uncontrollably. "P-p-please can we go back down?"

"What just did that?" asked Mary, jumping onto a nearby cloud. "You were falling, and something lifted you onto this cloud."

"I-I-I don't know," Chris murmured. "Just felt like an enormous gust of wind..."

At that moment, the Potter sisters could hear sobbing. Not Chris's sobbing. Someone else.

"Do you hear that?" Maz said to her sisters.

"Y-yes," Mary said, looking around. "Where is it coming from?"

"Mary, you stay with Chris," said Maz. "There's someone else up here with us. I'm going to find out who it is."

Maz jumped onto the nearest cloud and walked across it, following the sound of the sobs. Mary jumped onto Chris's cloud, where she was on her knees, still shaking from her frightening plunge through the sky. Mary hugged her and offered her a biscuit.

"Isn't that your last one?" Chris whispered.

"Yes, it is," said Mary, gritting her teeth as she reluctantly handed over her last biscuit. "But you're my sister and you're upset."

"Thank you," said Chris. As she was about to bite into it, Mary snatched it back and bit off a large chunk – which happened to be most of it. She passed the tiny fragment that was left back to Chris.

"Here," said Mary. "You have the rest."

Chris laughed.

Meanwhile, Maz saw a bright light ahead. She continued jumping from cloud to cloud, following the light. The sobbing got louder as she did, but she still couldn't see anyone.

"Is anyone up here?" Maz called out.

"Yes," said a small voice, and the bright light started to shimmer. "I am."

"Who? Who's there?"

"I'm the Lady of the Skies," the voice replied, in between sobs.

Maz couldn't see a lady, but she realized that because the bright light shimmered each time the voice spoke, that the bright light *was* the Lady.

"Are you the one who saved my sister from falling?" Maz asked gently.

"Yes," the Lady said. "That was me. I control the weather. The wind, the sun, the rain..."

"And the snow?"

"Yes. The snow is my doing. It is because I am sad and cannot stop weeping. And it's cold – always cold – because I am cold inside."

Maz realized that her mother was right. "It's been winter ever since I was born," said Maz. "You've been hurting all this time?"

"Yes."

"But why?"

"Because all the people in East Pudding are suffering."

Maz frowned. "East Pudding? Where's that? I've never heard of East Pudding!"

"It's on the other side of Pudding Woods," the Lady explained. "It's not like West Pudding. Everyone in West Pudding has everything they want and need – and more. But no one in East Pudding has anything."

"Really?"

"Yes. Everyone there is poor and hungry. They have no money, no food. They are sad and miserable. And each day one of them dies from the hunger."

"That sounds horrible. Especially as my village is so rich."

"You should go and see what it is like for yourself," the Lady suggested. "Go and see how they are living. You will be shocked."

"I think I will," Maz said. "Thank you for telling me."

Maz went back to meet her sisters. "Let's go," she said, jumping back across the clouds towards where the highest branches of the Sky Tree were poking through a large, hat-shaped cloud.

"Go where?" said Mary, taking Chris's hand and helping her to jump across the clouds.

"East Pudding," Maz replied.

"*East* Pudding?"

"Come," Maz said, as she started climbing down the Sky Tree. "I'll tell you on the way."

Chapter Five
A Village in Need

At this time of year, the days were short. By the time Maz, Chris and Mary were on their way to East Pudding, the sun was already setting. It made the snowflakes glow orange, as if the sky was raining down shavings of orange peel.

The Potter Sisters had never been through Pudding Woods before. Queen Murmur said they were off-limits. Right now the sisters were disobeying their queen, except that they didn't care. If there were people on the other side of the woods who needed help, they weren't going to just stand by and ignore them. Helping the people of East Pudding might even cheer up the Lady of the Skies, and finally put an end to the snow.

They trudged through the thick snow and dark, scary-looking trees, and eventually saw lights in the distance.

They arrived in a dreary, lifeless village, where no flowers bloomed and even the trees drooped in sadness. They looked in through the windows of some of the houses and saw families sitting down for lunch. Nobody was smiling and most families had a few slices of bread and a tiny handful of beans to go around four, maybe five of them. One family had a single, skinny-looking carrot which the mother had to slice up and share around her six children. Another family had a pot boiling on the stove. But all that was in it was water with two or three cabbage leaves.

Not very tasty.

Maz felt a tear trickle down her face as she watched.

Everyone in East Pudding wore thin, brown, raggedy clothes that were full of holes and looked like they hadn't been washed in ages. The houses were plain and dull inside – no decorations, ornaments or pictures, and very little furniture.

The Potter sisters made their way across the village square to the castle on the other side of East Pudding. It was similar to Queen Murmur's castle – but a lot smaller.

"Hello?" they called as they went inside, meeting only darkness. Nobody answered. They climbed up a swirling staircase, realizing as they went that each of the steps had eyes. But – like the rest of the village – they looked sleepy and sad.

Maz, Chris and Mary found a throne room at the top of the stairs. Inside was a collection of magical objects. A chair with a face. A table with a face. A cookie jar and an alarm clock, both with arms and legs. But like the steps, all of them looked sad, lost and hopeless.

36

And sitting – or more precisely slumped – on the throne was a man who looked like a wizard. He was just as sad and lost as the others and had his chin in his hands. He didn't even notice the Potter sisters enter his throne room.

"This is horrible," Chris whispered, wiping a tear from her cheek. "I don't want to see any more of this."

"We need to do something about this," Maz whispered to her sisters. She motioned for Chris and Mary to follow her out of the throne room. Nobody noticed them leave, just as nobody had seen them come in.

"But what?" asked Mary, as the three sisters clambered back down the steps and left the castle. "What are we going to do?"

Maz smiled and winked. "I have an idea."

Chapter Six
A Visit to the Bank

Maz, Mary and Chris made their way back through Pudding Woods to West Pudding. Maz took her sisters to the West Pudding Bank, just as it was about to close for the evening.

"Maz, what are we doing?" Mary asked her sister.

"We're helping East Pudding," said Maz. "That's what we're doing."

Maz walked over to the desk of Mr Weenie, who was busily counting coins. Chris and Mary followed. Mr Weenie was the head banker and one of the richest – and greediest – people in West Pudding.

"I'd like to withdraw my money, please," said Maz.

"What?" said Mr Weenie. "All of it?"

"Yes, all of it," said Maz. "I don't need it."

"I'd like to do the same," said Mary.

"Yes, and me too," Chris chimed in.

Mr Weenie frowned. "Do your parents know about this? I'm not sure your mother would be happy that—"

"All of us are old enough," Maz interrupted. "We don't need Mother's permission."

"May I ask why?" Mr Weenie pried.

"No, you may not," Maz snapped. "Now please hurry up."

"Y-yes, ma'am."

Mr Weenie set about emptying the three sisters' bank accounts. They asked for the money to be bundled together.

Mr Weenie handed Maz a bag containing nearly a thousand gold coins, which she hid beneath her coat.

"Thank you very much," said Maz, and the Potter sisters left the bank.

"Mmmm," murmured Mr Weenie suspiciously as they left.

"What is it, sir?" asked Reeves, his personal servant crow, perched on his shoulder.

"I'm not certain," replied Mr Weenie. "But there's something fishy going on. I can smell it."

"Can I do anything, sir?"

"You can, yes. You can get a message to Queen Murmur. Tell her the Potter sisters are up to something..."

Chapter Seven
A Good Deed Goes Wrong

Maz, Chris and Mary popped back home so that Mary could grab a pack of iced buns to eat on the journey. She did feel a bit guilty – since everyone in East Pudding had nothing to eat but a couple of beans – but she just couldn't help herself. Plus, she knew that everyone in East Pudding was about to be much better off. The sisters planned to hand out their gold coins to all of the families in East Pudding.

With the bag of gold coins still in Maz's coat, the three sisters ventured into Pudding Woods. The sun had set now, and silvery moonlight sliced through the trees, lighting up the snowflakes that were still falling. The darkness of the woods didn't discourage the three girls. There was no way they were going to allow the two villages to carry on as they had been. Not for a moment longer.

"Do you think Queen Murmur knows about East Pudding?" Chris asked Maz as they went.

"If she did, surely she would help them out," Maz reasoned.

"Yes, that's true. I'm sure she would if she knew," said Chris.

Just then, a great wind whipped and whistled through the trees. The three sisters spun around.

"Your Majesty!" cried Mary with a mouthful of iced bun. She dropped to her knees and bowed her head.

As Queen Murmur stepped out from between the trees, her silky black cloak rippling on the air, Chris and Maz also dropped to their knees.

"Rise, children," said Murmur with an icy glare.

Mary, Maz and Chris rose to their feet. Chris cowered in fear behind Maz. "What brings you out here, Your Majesty?" Maz asked.

"I might ask you the same question," Murmur growled, glistening snowflakes falling off her sharp, slick hair. "I thought I told everyone not to enter these woods. What are you up to?"

Mary shivered. She still hadn't swallowed her iced bun (because she'd stuffed far too much of it into her mouth), so she replied in a garbled voice, "We found this village on the other side of Pudding Woods."

"What? Try swallowing first, girl!" snapped Murmur.

"Sorry, Your Majesty," Maz stepped in. "What my sister said was, we found this village on the other side of the woods."

"Yes, East Pudding," said Murmur. "What of it?"

"Oh – you know about it?"

"Of course I do. My brother, Mumble, rules over it."

Maz remembered the sad-looking wizard she saw at the castle. So he's Murmur's brother! she realized. "But do you know how poor they are over there?" Maz asked.

"Yes. I made them that way."

"What?!" Maz felt anger rise from the pit of her stomach.

"I made East Pudding poor so I could make West Pudding rich," said Murmur.

"But why? Why would you want to do that?"

"What do you mean 'why'? Before I made East Pudding poor, West Pudding wasn't rich or powerful. Now we are both. Now everyone in West Pudding has everything they need – and more. Don't tell me you haven't enjoyed all your expensive toys and clothes and rich foods."

Murmur looked at Mary, who had just swallowed her iced bun but still had a ring of sugar around her mouth. "I know you have," she continued. "You couldn't have had all that if I hadn't made West Pudding rich. We look after ourselves first. That's what I've always taught you."

"There's no harm in trying to look after others as well," Maz argued. "Yes, we enjoy what we have. But we didn't know there was a village on the other side of the woods with nothing. We didn't know any different."

"That's why we wanted to help," squeaked Chris in her tiny voice, still partly hidden behind Maz.

"What was that, little one?" said Murmur. "You wanted to what?"

"Help..." Chris whispered.

Murmur's eyes sparked with rage. "Help?!"

"Yes," said Maz. "We took all our money out of our bank accounts and we're going to give it to everyone in East Pudding, to help them get back on their feet."

"Oh, really?"

"Yes, really." Maz had lost all respect for her queen, now that she knew Murmur was responsible for the people of East Pudding going hungry. It wasn't right and Maz wasn't going to stand for it.

"You should help us," Maz continued, "considering this is all your fault."

"Maz, sssshhh!" cried Mary. "That's the queen you're talking to!"

"I don't care if she's the queen," replied Maz defiantly. "She did this, and it was wrong. So she should help us put it right."

"Oh, I'll help you," hissed Murmur.

"You will?" said Maz.

"Yes, I will. I'll help all of you."

The Potter sisters huddled together and smiled. They were glad to have persuaded Queen Murmur to do the right thing. "Thank you, Your Majesty," said Maz.

"You're welcome," Murmur replied. She looked at Mary. "Let's start with you, shall we? You definitely need some help. You're the fattest little girl I've ever seen!"

"Wait – what?" cried Maz.

Murmur tutted. "How about I help you become a bit thinner, child? Would you like that?" Murmur took out her wand from beneath the folds of her cloak. She pointed the wand at Mary and golden sparkles began to spray from its tip and rain down over her.

For a moment, nothing happened. Then Mary's plump, round body began to change shape right in front of her sisters' horrified eyes.

Murmur's spell was certainly making Mary thinner – but not in the way you'd expect. It was flattening her!

"Murmur – stop!" shrieked Maz.

While Mary screamed, it looked to her sisters like her whole body was being squashed flat like a pancake – as if someone was rolling backwards and forwards over her with a giant rolling pin.

Soon Mary was lying on the ground, flat as a piece of paper. A colourful piece of paper, thanks to Mary's dress, which had blue and pink stripes and was covered in stars. She was still alive, but barely. She could just about blink her eyes as she looked up her terrified sisters. Chris started crying.

"Don't cry, little one," Murmur whispered. "I can help you too! Gosh, you're just so small, aren't you? Wouldn't you like to be bigger? Wouldn't you like to be a LOT bigger?"

Murmur waved her wand, raining golden sparkles down over Chris, which immediately began to stretch poor Chris's body.

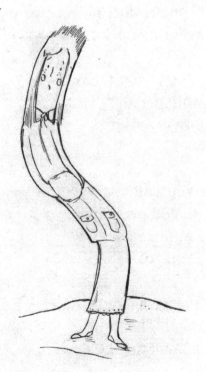

It stretched her and stretched her, longer and longer, till Chris's arms and legs were too long and thin to work anymore, and she collapsed onto the snowy ground.

Still the spell stretched her more and more, till she looked like a long piece of ribbon.

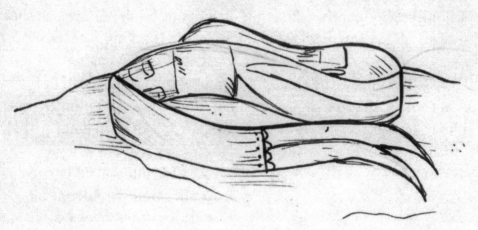

Murmur turned to Maz. "And you... what a scruff-bag you are! Your hair, my dear, looks like birds are nesting in there. And you clearly don't appreciate the expensive clothes your parents bought for you. Look at all the rips in them! Look at all the dirt! I can help you appreciate them. I can help you be a bit tidier, a bit less messy."

"Please don't," Maz whimpered. "Please turn my sisters back."

"You said you wanted my help," Murmur spat evilly. "You got it."

She waved her wand. The same shimmering golden

sparkles surged from the tip and rained down over Maz's head. Immediately her body started to change shape. Her belly swelled, her head sunk into her shoulders, her arms stuck to her sides and her legs rolled up into her belly and disappeared. For a  moment, she was a huge ball, but eventually sides and corners formed, and Maz turned into a box.

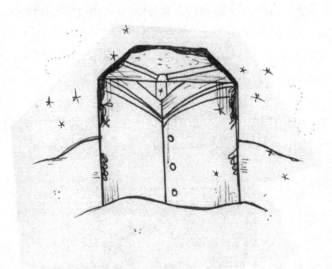

Murmur grinned wickedly, as Maz's frightened little eyes looked up at her from the lid of the box. "Much better," Murmur said. "Boxes keep mess hidden. Boxes keep clutter out of sight."

Laughing jubilantly, Murmur turned and headed back through the woods to West Pudding, satisfied that she had taught the Potter sisters a very valuable lesson about how stupid it is to be generous.

Meanwhile, the three sisters couldn't speak to each other, but they all knew that they weren't going to last very long in this state. They needed to find help, but they couldn't move very well. Maz was legless, Mary was like a sheet of paper with eyes, and Chris could only slither like a snake.

Still, they did what they could. Maz tried to shuffle closer to her sisters. She was eventually able to roll her box-shaped body into the centre of a flattened Mary. Chris slithered over to them and was able to lift Mary's paper-thin, stripy sides up and over Maz. With Mary draped around Maz, like a box wrapped in paper, Chris burrowed into the snow beneath her sisters and slithered up the sides of the 'box', tying herself into a little bow on top. That way – all three of them huddled together and cuddling one another – they could keep each other warm.

Maz closed her eyes and tried to sleep, hoping that someone would find them soon...

Chapter Eight
Mr and Mrs Fraggle

It wasn't long before Mr and Mrs Potter had realised that Maz, Mary and Chris had snuck out of the house. Mr Potter decided that the three girls had probably just gone to the park in West Pudding to play, so they waited a while for them to return.

Hours later, when there was still no sign of the girls, Mr and Mrs Potter decided to throw on coats and scarves and have a look around the village and the park. When they didn't find them, they began knocking on residents' doors.

Only one person had seen Mary, Maz and Chris. His name was Arthur Nicholas. He said he'd seen the sisters run to the bank and then head towards Pudding Woods. He also said he saw Queen Murmur enter the woods a short while later.

"What could they possibly be up to?" Mrs Potter asked her husband.

"I don't know, darling," said Mr Potter. "But if Queen Murmur went into the woods – which she never does – then she must've been following the girls. I reckon she knows where they are."

"Yes, maybe," Mrs Potter agreed. "You go to Queen Murmur's castle and find out. In the meantime, I'll go to Pudding Woods and continue searching for the girls myself."

"Are you sure you'll be okay?" said Mr Potter.

"I'll be fine," she assured him.

So Mr Potter trudged through the heavy snow to Murmur's castle, while Mrs Potter headed for the woods...

Meanwhile, Mr and Mrs Fraggle – an old-ish husband and wife from East Pudding – were making their way through Pudding Woods in the hope of finding help. Things had been really bad in East Pudding for a long time, but Mr and Mrs Fraggle had always managed to scrape by. Now they had literally run out of food. They had eaten half each of their very last slice of bread that evening and their cupboards were bare.

Suddenly, in middle of the woods, they came across a box wrapped in stripy, pink and blue paper, tied with a ribbon into a bow. Even though heavy snow had been falling for some time, a huge, sprawling tree had sheltered the box from the snow.

"Oooo!" cried Mrs Fraggle. "Look, Mr Fraggle! What's this?"

"Mmmm," wondered Mr Fraggle, one eyebrow raised. "I'm not sure, Mrs Fraggle. But it looks most appealing, doesn't it?"

Mrs Fraggle bent down and inspected the mysterious box. She was a little bit short-sighted, so she couldn't see that there were two little pairs of eyes, one pair in the wrapping paper, one pair in the ribbon. But all four eyes were shut, which made noticing them even more unlikely.

Mrs Fraggle lifted the box off the ground. It was heavy and made a tinkling noise as she picked it up. "There's something inside it, Mr Fraggle."

"It's a package of some kind, Mrs Fraggle," said her husband. "Do you think we should open it?"

"Yes, Mr Fraggle. I think we should."

So Mrs Fraggle untied the bow and removed the ribbon, which she handed to her husband. Then she unwrapped the box from the wrapping paper. The box itself was a bit tatty and dirty – and again Mrs Fraggle didn't notice that there was a little pair of eyes in the lid. But just like the eyes in the ribbon and the paper, they were shut.

Mrs Fraggle gently shook the box. They heard lots of tinkling and chinking inside, like lots of little pieces of metal knocking together.

"Open it, Mrs Fraggle," said Mr Fraggle.

Mrs Fraggle lifted the lid off the box. Inside was a big green bag of – well – something. She lifted the bag out of the box and handed it to her husband. He opened the bag, looked inside and his eyes widened – so wide in fact that they nearly fell out of his head.

"What is it, Mr Fraggle? What's in there?"

"Gold coins, Mrs Fraggle. Lots of them. There must be close to a thousand in this bag."

"A *thousand*? That's – but that's enough to feed everyone in East Pudding! And repair the poisoned crop fields! I – I don't believe it! Mr Fraggle, who could have left these here?"

At that moment, Mr and Mrs Fraggle could hear Mrs Potter in the distance. Mrs Potter was searching for her children and calling out their names at the top of her voice: "Mary! Chris! Maz!"

"Did you hear that, Mr Fraggle?" asked Mrs Fraggle.

Mrs Potter called their names again, "Mary! Chris! Maz!"

"Yes, Mrs Fraggle, I can hear that," answered Mr Fragglc. "What do you think shc's shouting?"

Mrs Fraggle listened. Mrs Potter called again, "Mary! Chris! Maz!"

"It sounds like 'Me-rry-Chris-Mass', Mr Fraggle. Merry Christmas."

"Merry Chris-what?"

Mrs Fraggle listened again. "MARY! CHRIS! MAZ!"

"Yes," said Mrs Fraggle. "It's 'Merry Christmas'. Whoever she is, she's wishing us a 'Merry Christmas'."

"What's 'Christmas'?" wondered Mr Fraggle curiously.

"Maybe that's what this box of gold coins is all about, Mr Fraggle," Mrs Fraggle reasoned. "Maybe it's a celebration of some kind. A celebration called Christmas."

"You mean you think these coins are a gift, Mrs Fraggle?"

"They must be! They were right here for us to find, inside a box that's been deliberately wrapped in decorative paper and tied with a pretty ribbon. It's a gift, a present, and now there's a woman shouting 'Merry Christmas' to us. It's obviously some kind of holiday we've not experienced before, Mr Fraggle."

"Yes!" cried Mr Fraggle with a gleeful smile. "That makes perfect sense, Mrs Fraggle!"

Mrs Potter shouted again, "MARY! CHRIS! MAZ!"

So Mrs Fraggle thought it only polite to call back, "Thank you! And a Merry Christmas to you too!"

Chapter Nine
The Fall of West Pudding

On the other side of the woods, Mrs Potter didn't hear Mrs Fraggle shout, "Merry Christmas." She had broken down in tears next to a tree, worried and upset that she still hadn't found her daughters. She decided to head back to West Pudding to see if her husband had had any luck with Murmur.

Realizing that her husband had not yet come back from Murmur's castle, Mrs Potter decided to go there herself. When she arrived, she heard raised voices coming from Murmur's throne room and raced up the stairs.

Murmur and her husband were arguing, but Mrs Potter wasn't sure what about. "How could you do that? You're evil! An evil witch!" Mr Potter was shouting.

"Don't you dare speak to me like that, you hideous, hairy beanpole!" Murmur snarled back. "I did it for their own good! They needed to be punished for being so stupid!"

"What?" cried Mrs Potter as she entered the throne room. "What did she do?"

"She... k-killed them..." Mr Potter said, his voice cracking, tears filling his eyes. "She killed our daughters..."

"WHAT?!" screamed Mrs Potter.

"They might not be dead yet!" Murmur pointed out. "But... well, they probably are."

"How c-could you?!" Mrs Potter shrieked.

"Murmur told me they were trying to give money to the people of East Pudding, a poor village on the other side of Pudding Woods," said Mr Potter, crying. "So she had to teach them a lesson."

Mrs Potter hugged her husband, tears streaming from her eyes.

"I could've lied to the both of you," Murmur said. "I could've told you I'd not seen Mary, Chris or Maz. But I've told you the truth so that both of you can learn from this."

"LEARN from this?" cried Mrs Potter.

"Yes," said Murmur. "Learn that being generous to others less fortunate than you is not the answer. If you want to stay rich and powerful and secure, you need to look after yourself first. Just as I've always taught you."

"We didn't know there was another village out there," said Mrs Potter. "If we did, and if we knew that they were poorer than us, we would've done just what our girls tried to do. We would've helped."

"Then you are fools."

"You're wrong, Murmur. You're the fool. Just you wait and see."

Mr and Mrs Potter stormed out of Murmur's throne room and left the castle. Murmur looked into her cauldron, filled with a blood-coloured liquid that could show her images of what was happening in West and East Pudding. She watched as Mr and Mrs Potter went and knocked on the doors of other residents in West Pudding.

She couldn't hear what they were saying, because the cauldron only showed her pictures. But she could see that many of the residents, after speaking with Mr and Mrs Potter, were gathering up items – bangles, necklaces, coins, cakes and toys – and putting them in boxes. Then they were wrapping them in paper and ribbons.

Murmur knew what they were doing. They were preparing gifts for the people of East Pudding – just like Mary, Chris and Maz had done.

Not all of the residents were joining in. Some of the greedier residents were not interested in helping East Pudding. But what Murmur was shocked to discover was that most people in the village *were* preparing to give presents to East Pudding.

"After everything I've taught them," Murmur snarled, rage bubbling inside her. "Everything I've done for them – and they go and do THIS!"

As her rage boiled over, black lightning fizzed and sparked at her fingertips. She overturned her cauldron, spilling red liquid all over the marble floor of her throne room. She grabbed one of her vultures and throttled it, chucking its dead body against the wall with a crack.

"Vultures! Crows!" she called to all of the rest of her servants. "Bring them to me! All of them! Everyone in West Pudding! Lock them in the lower dungeon! Now!"

Before the West Pudding residents were able to deliver their presents to the people of East Pudding, huge flocks of crows and vultures had descended on the village. They clutched all the residents in their beaks, swept them up into the sky and dragged them to the lower dungeon of Murmur's castle. Even the greedy ones were taken, the ones who Murmur used to call friends.

Before long, the houses of West Pudding were empty. Mr and Mrs Potter, Arthur Nicholas, Mr Weenie and all the rest of the people of West Pudding were piled into cages in the lower dungeon.

Murmur decided that she couldn't trust any of them. Not

anymore. Only one person was given a reprieve. Mr Weenie.
He was the one who told Murmur about Mary, Chris and Maz.
So Murmur let him out of his cage and he became her most
trusted servant.

Murmur's first job for Mr Weenie was to oversee the
destruction of West Pudding, to organise a force of vultures and
crows to burn down all the houses in the village. They weren't
needed anymore. Mr Weenie did as he was told. He even
burned down his own house.

Murmur watched from her throne room as West Pudding was engulfed in flames. The snow started to fall harder, drowning the flames that were ravaging the village, putting the fire out. But West Pudding was already a huge pile of ash.

"You're too late, Mother," whispered Murmur evilly. "I have won."

Chapter Ten
The First Christmas

Meanwhile, Mr and Mrs Fraggle had placed the bag of gold coins back into the box, re-wrapped it in the stripy paper, and re-tied the bow. They had hurried back to East Pudding, excitement tinkling through their bones.

By the time they arrived back in the village, the sun was just starting to rear its head. It was dawn, December 25th, a new day. And what a day it was going to be.

See, what Murmur didn't know was that Maz still had the bag of gold coins in her coat when she transformed into a box. Because the spell was meant for Maz – not for any objects she was carrying – the bag of coins didn't transform. It just ended up inside the box.

Mr and Mrs Fraggle took the box of coins straight to Mumble and explained what had happened in the woods. They let him unwrap the present just as they had done. As soon as Mumble cast his eyes upon the glinting coins, his whole manner changed. He smiled – something he hadn't done for years. He laughed – something he'd nearly forgotten how to do. Then he leapt off his throne, ran around the room, jumped up and down and danced the hokey cokey with Mable the table and Bumfy the comfy chair. The rest of his magical companions – Drop the cookie jar, Alumi and Copps the saucepan sisters, and the rabbits from his garden – rejoiced with him.

East Pudding was saved.

As the morning sun rose in the sky, Mumble left his castle and handed out the gold coins to all the families in the village. Overjoyed, the villagers flooded into Mrs Carter's shop and bought bread, cheese, meat, potatoes and eggs. Mrs Carter was delighted. She had not had much business lately, and her shelves didn't have much food on them because she couldn't afford more stock. But before midday, the villagers had cleared all the food she did have off her shelves. So she immediately had to order more.

Mr Raggalaggerlooof, East Pudding's farmer, now had enough money to buy materials to build a machine that would suck up all the poison from the crop fields. For years he'd been growing really small amounts of crops in patches where the poison hadn't quite reached. Now Mr Raggalaggerlooof could repair all the fields and start growing wheat and corn in large quantities like he used to.

Tiberius Twinkle's toy-making business started up again. Everyone wanted to buy toys – even the grown-ups! There was also new demand for sweets, which delighted the village candymaker Timothy Twinkle. He was very thankful to be busy again. Mrs Mistle was pleased too. Now she had enough money to buy seedlings to grow fruits, flowers and vegetables in her garden, and make pies and cakes for the village – just like she once did.

Sadly, Mary, Chris and Maz had not survived the cold in their new forms. Their little eyes were shut forever, and no one would know that the 'present' used to be three little girls. But their gold coins had found their way to East Pudding just as they intended. Their message of hope lived on.

And it wasn't just that they'd saved East Pudding. They had also brought 'Christmas' to East Pudding – something they *hadn't* intended.

From that point on, the people of East Pudding would celebrate Christmas on December 25th by giving gifts to each other. And just like the very first present that Mr and Mrs Fraggle had discovered in Pudding Woods, they would conceal the gifts in boxes, wrap the boxes in colourful paper and tie them with ribbons and bows. Each Christmas they would sing words of thanks to the mysterious gift-giver who had saved their village and given them their lives back, and they would promise never to forget.

And they never did.

Chapter Eleven
Time for Bed...and Granny's Secret

"There you have it, my darlings," said Granny. "That is how Christmas started."

Georgina laughed. "So it was actually Murmur who brought Christmas to East Pudding!"

"Accidentally, yes," said Granny. "She never understood what 'Christmas' was, and she never realized that it was all because of her. All she knew was that she hated it. And she was going to put a stop to it, which, as you know, she ultimately failed to do."

"But wait!" cried George. "What happened to the people of West Pudding? Did they ever get to give presents to the people of East Pudding like they wanted? Were they ever free of Murmur?"

Granny smiled. "George, my love, you already know the answers to those questions."

"We do?" Georgina chimed in.

"Yes, my darlings. I told you before how Murmur kept the people of West Pudding in her dungeon for years until she found a use for them. One day, she did. After her accident with the Ultimate Blender, which turned her half-scorpion, she used her new scorpion sting to transform all the people of West Pudding into her evil elves."

"Oh, yes!" cried Georgina, remembering. "Like Atnas!"

"Yes, and do you remember what happened to Atnas, the elf who used to be Arthur Nicholas? Do you remember what happened after he turned back into a person and became Santa Claus?"

"Yes – I do!" said George. "Mumble and Murmur had their final battle, and Murmur fell into a giant crack in the Earth and was killed. That's right, isn't it?"

"Yes, George, that's right. And when that happened, all the elves in Murmur's castle turned back into people and were free. That's when they decided to continue their plans to bring presents, just as they had planned to do before Murmur kidnapped them and locked them away. That's when – instead of being Murmur's 'elves' – they became Santa's 'elves'. Even today, the people of West Pudding are still helping Santa make and deliver presents to all the children of the world."

Mum decided she had heard enough. "Granny, are you telling porky-pies to my children?" she said with a smirk. "Surely that can't all be true? You're telling us that Christmas only started because of a present that was actually, well, the bodies of three little girls, and because an old man and woman misheard their mother calling their names?"

"Er – well, yes," Granny smiled. "What do you believe, my dear?"

Mum looked at George and Georgina, eagerly waiting for her answer, and winked. "I believe..." she said softly, "... that it's time for bed!"

"Ooooh, Mum!" cried George and Georgina together with disappointment.

"Your mother's right," Granny agreed. "Santa will be here shortly."

If it was any other night, George and Georgina might protest, but they knew that Santa only visited houses with sleeping children. Granny had said so in her very first Christmas story. So the two children kissed Mum and Dad and Granny goodnight and started up the stairs to bed.

Then George stopped. "Is East Pudding still out there somewhere, Granny? Does it still exist?"

"Oh, I don't think so, George," Granny said. "It was a very long time ago."

George nodded sadly and carried on up the stairs.

"See you tomorrow, children," said Granny. "And Merry Christmas."

Georgina formed a sad look. "You mean, Mary, Chris, Maz..."

"Indeed," said Granny. "And that is why we'll always remember them."

"Night, Granny," said George and Georgina together. "Merry Christmas."

George and Georgina climbed into bed and watched the glistening snowfall through the window, counting the snow-flakes as they drifted off to sleep. Downstairs, Mum and Dad put Dipstick to bed and brewed themselves some hot chocolate.

Meanwhile, Granny did all of her last-minute checks for Christmas Day.

She checked that by the fireplace was a mince pie and a glass of sherry for Santa – the things which caused Atnas to remember who he really was.

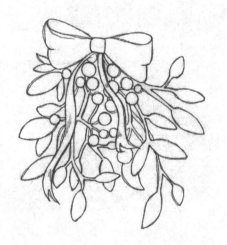

She made sure there was mistletoe hanging above every doorway in memory of the half-human, half-plant Mrs Mistle and her kissing habit.

She checked that all the places were set at the dinner table, with plates, cutlery and – of course – Christmas crackers. To remember the Twinkles and their escape from the Giants.

She made sure that all the fairy lights on the Christmas tree were twinkling. That the fairy on top was secure, protecting the presents beneath – just like Celeste and her children had protected Podney Tiptoe.

And finally she checked the presents at the foot of the tree, making sure they were all wrapped, remembering the Potter sisters, their kindness, and how they had huddled together to keep warm in the snow.

Then she kissed Mum and Dad goodnight and headed home to her own house to get some sleep before the big day. Granny lived with Grandad and Uncle Rusty on the other side of Dandiest Pug. It was only a short walk away.

Granny's path took her past the sign for "Dandiest Pug", and – as always – she smiled knowingly when she saw it. It was a very old sign. Granny could still see the lines from where it had been glued back together.

You see, many, many years ago – centuries in fact – the Dandiest Pug sign was damaged in a storm. Smashed to bits. Each letter of the village name had been sucked up by the wind and strewn across the nearest field. It was a long, long time before anyone thought to repair the sign, but by the time they did, they'd forgotten what the village used to be called. So they gathered up the broken letters, arranged them to make "D A N D I E S T P U G", and glued them back together.

Granny hadn't been telling porkies about where Christmas came from, but when George asked if East Pudding still existed, and Granny said she didn't think so, that WAS a porky.

Because only Granny knew what Dandiest Pug used to be called. Only she knew what the sign used to read. She'd always known. It was a secret that had been a part of her family for generations.

It used to read "E A S T P U D D I N G".

ALL THE BOOKS IN
THE EAST PUDDING CHRONICLES

The Christmas Monster

The Merry Mrs Mistle

Tale of the Twinkles

Plight of the Witch Watchers

The First Christmas

ABOUT THE AUTHOR

Christopher hopes you've enjoyed reading *The East Pudding Chronicles* as much as he's enjoyed writing them. It took him quite some time to come up with the idea for *The First Christmas* and make it a worthy end to the series. He hopes that with Mary, Chris and Maz, he found a nice balance between 'magical' and 'dark', because that's what he's always aimed for with *The East Pudding Chronicles*.

He's also glad to have put in some references to Tim Burton's *The Nightmare Before Christmas* – the original inspiration for this series!

Hopefully you enjoyed all the twists and turns in this final book. They've been long in the making! (Did anyone guess Dandiest Pug's big secret?)

Christopher is sad to be leaving behind George and Georgina, Mumble and Murmur and all the characters that have come alive on these pages thanks to Emily's delightful drawings.

He would like to thank his readers, his friends and family for their support, and Emily for all of her wonderful creations.

Merry Christmas to all, and to all a good night.

ABOUT THE ILLUSTRATOR

Devastated when she didn't receive her Hogwarts letter, Emily decided to do something just as magical so decided to illustrate and write children's books instead! She has worked on a number of other children's books, both writing her own stories and illustrating for other authors. More of her work can be seen at www.emilyharperillustration.co.uk.

Emily works as an illustrator and animator as well as being the artist in residence for a local school. This means she gets to spend lots of time with the most imaginative people there are – children!

Emily can't believe this is the last book in the series, and will miss her yearly adventures with George, Georgina and co!